"For my godson, may you always
I love you."

First B3 printing May 2023

Published in Lansing, Michigan

Visit www.booksbuildingback.com

Library of Congress Cataloging-in-Publication Data
Name: John, Kenneth, author, illustrator.
Title: Smile Miles / by Kenneth John
Audience: Ages 3-8
Summary: "A little boy, who decides to stop smiling, tries other gestures to express his happiness."
Identifiers: LCCN 2022920187(print)
ISBN 978-1-960467-13-3

Printed in the USA

Smile Miles

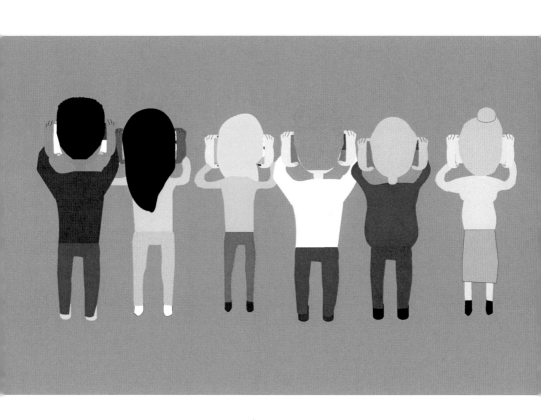

Written and illustrated
by Kenneth John

As early as he could remember everyone was always telling Miles to smile.

Smile Miles!

Miles didn't understand why everyone kept telling him to smile. He felt like he was already smiling.

The more people who told Miles to smile, the harder he would try.

The harder he tried,
the more people said
Smile Miles!

After years and years of smiling bigger and bigger Miles' face hurt.

Eventually, Miles just stopped smiling.

He didn't smile at parties.

Smile Miles!

He didn't smile
on the phone.

He didn't even smile
when playing.

Smile Miles!

Even though Miles didn't smile anymore he was still a happy boy. Miles decided he would try other gestures to express his happiness.

He once heard that a great smile started with the eyes so he thought he would try that. But every time Miles tried widening his eyes in delight people thought something was wrong.

Next, he thought he would try a thumbs up. But people would always respond with "He likes it" or "that's good". Miles wasn't looking for approval to be happy. He was just happy.

Finally, he tried making heart hands to express his happiness but that just didn't feel right.

When Miles stopped smiling, he noticed those around him stopped smiling too.

Miles' family and friends didn't know how to respond to his wide eyes, thumbs up or heart hands. They missed Miles' smile.

Most of all, Miles missed everyone smiling back at him.

Miles realized that smiling not only made him happy but it made everyone around him happy.

He also realized nothing
felt better
than a smile.

And that's just what he did.

Smile Miles!